Mystery by Moonlight

Terrified of what he would see, Norman forced himself across the yard toward Marcel's doghouse. The closer he got to the tree, the slower he moved. He took the last few steps feeling as if his sneakers were made of lead.

"AW-OOO!"

"Yipes!" The sound was so close, and so loud, that the creature had to be practically on top of him.

Suddenly, from out of the shadows behind the doghouse, *something* came streaking toward Norman. The creature sprang toward him. It was lean and hairy and its eyes gleamed green-gold in the moonlight.

The werewolf!

NORMAN NEWMAN
and the Werewolf of Walnut Street

NORMAN NEWMAN
and the Werewolf of Walnut Street

ELLEN CONFORD
illustrated by Tim Jacobus

little rainbow®
Troll Associates

10 9 8 7 6 5 4 3 2 1

Library of Congress Cataloging-in-Publication Data

Conford, Ellen.
Norman Newman and the werewolf of Walnut Street / by Ellen
Conford; illustrated by Tim Jacobus.
p.   cm.—(Norman Newman)
Summary: Norman is temporarily distracted from his suspicions
about his sister, the "Evil Elaine," when his imagination runs wild
with worries about a werewolf in the neighborhood.
ISBN 0-8167-3849-1 (lib.)   ISBN 0-8167-3719-3 (pbk.)
[1. Brothers and sisters—Fiction.   2. Werewolves—Fiction.
3. Family life—Fiction.]   I. Jacobus, Tim, ill.   II. Title.
III. Series: Conford, Ellen. Norman Newman
PZ7.C7593No   1995   [Fic]—dc20   95-12758

NORMAN NEWMAN
and the Werewolf of Walnut Street

CHAPTER 1

The howl slashed the moonlit night like a jagged knife.

Norman Newman sat up in bed, clutching the sheet under his chin. "What was that?" he whispered. He reached for his dog, Phil, who usually slept at the end of his bed. But Phil wasn't there.

"OWW-OOOO!"

It was the most hideous sound Norman had ever heard.

"Phil, where are you?" Norman looked around his room.

The moon made a little puddle of light on the floor beneath his window. There, in the middle of the pale circle, stood Phil.

His ears were pricked and his little stub of tail was quivering.

"It sounds like a wolf." Norman shivered. "I didn't know there were any wolves around here." He got out of bed and went to the window. "What do you see, boy?" he asked Phil.

But there was nothing to see. No one was out there. Certainly no wolves.

Maybe it was just a dream, Norman thought.

But if it was just a dream, Phil must have had the same dream. Because he was still standing, tense and alert, at the window, staring at the moonlight.

"AWWOOO-WOO-OOO!"

Norman and Phil dived for the bed at the same time. Norman jumped into it and pulled the covers over his head. Phil crawled under it and made little scratching sounds with his paws.

"We really ought to find out what that is," Norman said from under the covers. "There might be a dangerous . . . *something* loose in the neighborhood."

He pushed the covers back and leaned over the edge of his bed. "Come on out, Phil."

Phil crawled backward, farther under the bed, until he was pressed against the wall.

"You're probably right," said Norman. "Maybe we should wait until daylight to investigate."

But it wasn't going to be easy to get back to sleep.

Norman closed his eyes.

"I'm getting sleepy," he told himself. "I'm getting very, very sleepy."

"AWWOOO-WOO!"

"No, I'm not!" Norman turned on the light next to his bed. Maybe he ought to go wake his parents. They were probably up anyway. Who could possibly sleep through that horrible howling?

And if they were still asleep, he ought to warn them. Just in case there was a dangerous . . . *something* loose in the neighborhood.

He got out of bed and went down the hall. He knocked on their door softly. "Mom? Dad?"

"AWWOOO-WOO!"

"Yipes!" He flung the door open, and it banged back against the wall. Norman leaped for the bed and landed somewhere on top of his father.

"Oof!"

"Wake up!" said Norman. "I think there's a wolf outside."

"Norman, what in the world—"

"Didn't you hear it?"

"You mean the dog?" Norman's mother asked sleepily.

"Norman, would you get off my chest, please?" his father said.

"Sorry." Norman rolled sideways. "That was no dog," he said. "I've never heard anything like it."

"It was just a dog baying at the moon," said Mr. Newman. "Dogs do that."

"No dog around here does that," Norman said.

"Well, maybe someone has a new dog," his mother said.

"That was no dog," Norman insisted. "I think it was a wolf."

"Norman, your imagination is running wild again." His father sat up. "This is the suburbs. Where would a wolf have come from?"

"Maybe one escaped from the zoo," Norman suggested.

"There aren't any zoos around here," his mother said.

"Maybe it walked here from the zoo in the city," Norman said.

"If it did," said Mrs. Newman, "it'll be too tired to bother anybody."

Norman's father looked at the clock radio on the night table. "Norman, I have to fly to Cincinnati in six hours. I really need my sleep."

Mr. Newman was a computer consultant. He traveled a lot.

"If you want to stay here with us," his father went on, "that's okay. But you have to be quiet and go to sleep."

"Well . . ." Norman was scared, but he was too old to act like a baby. "Even if it is a wolf," he said, "it probably can't get into the house."

"Definitely not," his mother mumbled. "I locked the doors."

Norman went back to his room. Phil was curled up on his pillow, sleeping.

Whatever it was, it must be gone, Norman told himself. *Phil wouldn't have gone to sleep if we were in danger.*

He looked out the window. There was nothing in the street but a couple of parked cars and some trash cans.

He was about to turn away from the window when he saw it. The shadow appeared first, looming up from behind a garbage can across the street. It had a large head, a pointy snout, and four lean legs.

Norman gasped. He gripped the windowsill till his knuckles turned white.

He closed his eyes for a moment and took a deep breath to steady himself. *Whatever it is, it can't get in here,* he told himself.

He opened his eyes—just in time to see a long, gray . . . *thing* . . . slink across the street and disappear around the corner.

Norman backed away from the window. He swallowed a couple of times, trying to keep the fear down.

But he felt as if icy fingers were clutching his heart.

He crawled into bed and pulled Phil into his arms.

"Maybe it was just a dog," Norman whispered.

Phil snored softly.

"A hungry dog looking for something to eat," Norman went on. "Or maybe a regular dog from around here who had to go out."

Norman burrowed under the covers. "And even if it was a wolf, it couldn't get into the house. Mom locked all the doors."

He pulled the pillow down under the covers. Phil rolled over and wriggled under his arm.

"And even if it could get in here," Norman went on, "you wouldn't let it hurt me. Would you? Because you're Phil the Wonder Dog."

That's what Norman called him, because Phil was so smart.

Phil made a snuffling noise and nuzzled Norman's armpit.

"But it's probably not a wolf," Norman said. "Not a wolf. Not a—"

"AWW-OOOO-WOO!"

CHAPTER

2

At breakfast the next morning, the Evil Elaine lined up four tall glasses of water next to her toast.

Norman called his sister the Evil Elaine because she was so nasty to him.

"What are you doing with all that water?" Norman asked.

"Drinking it, stupid."

"Elaine, don't call your brother stupid," her mother said. "It's a reasonable question. I'm curious myself."

"Winona McCall drinks sixteen glasses of water a day," Elaine said. Winona McCall was Elaine's favorite movie star. Elaine wanted to be an actress, and she eagerly read every word she could find about her idol.

"Winona McCall says it flushes the poisons out of your system and makes your skin glow," she went on.

"Sixteen glasses of water a day must make for a lot of flushing," her father joked.

"Daddy, that's disgusting!" Elaine glared at him.

"You have poisons in your system?" Norman asked. He imagined an X-ray picture of Elaine's insides, with tiny little skulls and crossbones scurrying around in her veins.

"So I'm going to drink four glasses of water with breakfast," she said, ignoring Norman. "Four glasses with lunch, four glasses with dinner, and four glasses before I go to bed."

"And spend all night in the bathroom," added Mr. Newman.

"Father!"

Norman's mother was thumbing through the morning newspaper as she sipped her coffee.

"Is there anything in there about an escaped wolf?" Norman asked.

"No," said his mother, "and I'm sure it wasn't a wolf."

"What wasn't a wolf?" Elaine asked.

"Didn't you hear that howling last night?"

Norman couldn't believe it. How could she have slept through that horrible noise?

"I didn't hear anything," Elaine said. "You're probably imagining things. As usual."

"I am not!" Norman retorted. "Mom and Dad heard it too."

Elaine turned to her mother. "There was a wolf here last night?"

"It wasn't a wolf," Mrs. Newman insisted. "It was just a dog."

"Wow. It would be great if we did have a wolf in the neighborhood," Elaine said dreamily. "It could be our mascot We could use it in our demonstrations."

"What demonstrations?" Norman's father put down his coffee cup.

Elaine pulled something out of her pocket and pinned it onto her black tanktop. "Our anti-fur demonstrations," she said.

Norman leaned over to look at the large green button Elaine had pinned on. It said: Fur: Pet It, Don't Wear It.

She gulped down a glass of water and looked at her watch.

"We're having one at the mall today. I have to be there at ten o'clock."

"You're going to an anti-fur demonstration to-day?" her father asked. "Who's wearing fur in July?"

"Murray's Mansion of Mink is having a Christmas in July sale," Elaine said. She chugged down another glass of water. "Winona McCall got arrested in an anti-fur demonstration," Elaine went on, her eyes shining. "She was handcuffed and fingerprinted and everything."

Her mother put down the newspaper. "I hope you don't get arrested."

"Do you think I might?" Elaine asked hopefully.

"Doesn't anybody care about the wolf?" Norman said in a loud voice. "Even Phil the Wonder Dog was scared."

"Phil the Wonder Dog," sneered the Evil Elaine, "is scared of lint."

"That's not true!" Norman reached down under the table and scratched Phil's ears. Phil was a great dog, and very smart. Norman had once read a magazine article about canine intelligence. At the end of the article there was an IQ test you could give to your dog to see how bright he was. Phil could fetch, sit, lie down, beg, and shake paws. He would have scored "genius" on the dog IQ test, except that sometimes when you said, "Sit!" he held out his paw. And when you said, "Shake hands!" he rolled over on his back and stuck his legs up in the air.

"Well," said Mr. Newman, "I hate to break up this peaceful morning scene, but I have to get to the airport."

"I'm ready." Norman's mother folded up the newspaper. "Norman, do you want to come with us?"

Usually Norman liked to go to the airport, but today he was eager to finish the book he was reading.

"No, I'm almost at the end of *Red Fang, Dog of Darkness*."

"Again?" his mother said. "You must have read that book six times."

"Only four," said Norman.

"No wonder he thinks he hears wolves," said Elaine. "Every time he reads one of those Monroe Marlin books, his imagination goes berserk."

"And every time you read about Winona McCall, you do something dumb," he shot back.

"Jerk!" snapped Elaine.

"Jerkess," retorted Norman.

"I'm going to miss these sparkling intellectual discussions while I'm away," their father said.

When his parents left for the airport, Norman

21

went to his room to finish *Red Fang*. It was about Red, an Irish setter puppy that the hero, Timmy, saved from the dog pound. Strange, terrible things started to happen as Red grew up. All the pets in the neighborhood were afraid of him.

Then, one night, by the light of a full moon, Timmy watched in horror as his cute puppy transformed itself into a snarling wolf.

Norman shivered every time he read the description of the dog's dripping fangs and blood red eyes.

"I'm going to the mall now," Elaine yelled half an hour later. "You'd better go over to Milo's until Mom gets home."

"I haven't finished my book yet," Norman yelled back.

"You read it four times and you still don't know how it's going to end?" Elaine said. "You're dumber than I thought."

"I hope you do get arrested," Norman grumbled. But he closed the book and followed the Evil Elaine outside.

Norman's best friend, Milo Burgess, lived right next door. Norman rang the bell. Milo's father opened the door. He had a frying pan in one hand and was holding a spatula between his teeth.

"Hlo Nmn," he mumbled. He closed the door and took the spatula out of his mouth. "Come on in. We're just having breakfast."

Norman followed him into the kitchen. "So late?" he asked.

"A howling dog kept us up half the night," Mr. Burgess said.

Mrs. Burgess was making coffee. Milo was sitting at the kitchen table, his plate piled high with pancakes.

"Hi, Norman," said Mrs. Burgess. "Would you like some breakfast?"

"I had breakfast already," Norman said. He looked at Milo's pancakes. They glistened with syrup and golden pools of melting butter.

"But it was a very small breakfast," he added.

He sat down next to Milo's wheelchair. Mrs. Burgess got an extra plate and put it in front of Norman.

"One more order of Fred's Famous Flapjacks coming up," said Mr. Burgess. He swirled a lump of butter around in the frying pan.

"I don't think that was a dog last night," Norman said. "It sounded like a wolf."

"It couldn't have been a wolf," Milo's mother said.

Milo swallowed a mouthful of pancakes. "What makes you think it was a wolf?"

"I saw it," Norman said.

"You saw a wolf?" Mr. Burgess asked.

"Well, I didn't get a very close look," Norman admitted. "But it could have been a wolf."

Milo looked thoughtful. "It really did sound more like a wild animal than any dog I ever heard."

"But where would a wolf have come from?" his mother asked.

"Maybe it escaped from the zoo," said Norman. "I'm going to go looking for it after breakfast."

"Good idea," Milo said. "I'll go with you."

"If you find it," Milo's father said, "you'll have a great story to write about how you spent your summer vacation."

"I can't believe you believe me," Norman said, as Milo rolled his wheelchair down the ramp from the front door to the sidewalk. They had just finished breakfast. "Usually you say I'm imagining things."

"Usually you are," Milo said. "But I've got no plans for today and there's nothing on TV except reruns. And I never did hear a dog around here that sounded like that."

"Let's take Phil with us," Norman said. "If there's a wolf around here, he'll track him down."

Norman ran into his house. Phil was curled up under the kitchen table, snoring. Norman got Phil's leash.

"Come on, boy," he said, "we're going to catch a wolf."

Phil opened one eye, but he didn't move.

Norman crawled under the table and snapped the leash onto Phil's collar. "I know it's scary," he said, "but you're Phil the Wonder Dog. You're not afraid of anything, right, boy?"

Phil yawned and closed his eye.

"I guess you're tired," Norman said. "Okay, I'll carry you." He scooped Phil up, crawled out from under the table, and carried him outside.

"I'll show you where I saw him." Norman held onto the back of Milo's wheelchair so he could get down from the curb to the street without bouncing. Milo had been hurt in an auto accident when he was little. But he could get around well in his wheelchair.

"Right there." Norman led him across the street. "Near the garbage cans."

Milo shook his head. "Boy, what a mess." The lids were off the cans, and one can was tipped on its side. There were banana peels and ripped cereal boxes and stained coffee filters all over the sidewalk. At the sight of all that garbage, Phil's stubby tail quivered, and he tugged eagerly at the leash.

"The wolf must have been looking for something to eat," Norman said.

"Aw, Norman," Milo said, disappointed. "It's just the Rosenblooms' house."

"I know," Norman said. "This is where I saw him."

"But the Rosenblooms have a dog," Milo said. "He probably got out last night and went through the garbage."

"Marcel is a French poodle," Norman said. "He doesn't look like a wolf. He doesn't sound like a wolf."

"Maybe he was hungrier than usual," Milo suggested. "Let's clean this up, so Mrs. Rosenbloom and Mrs. Rosenbloom don't have to do it."

The Rosenblooms were twin sisters who had married twin brothers. When the brothers died, Mrs. Rosenbloom and Mrs. Rosenbloom had moved in together. They were pretty old. Mrs. Lana Rosenbloom walked with a cane, and Mrs. Lola Rosenbloom didn't hear too well.

Norman and Milo helped them out whenever they got a chance.

Milo bent over and turned the fallen garbage can right side up. He and Norman began picking up the garbage.

"It couldn't have been Marcel," Norman insisted. "Phil would have recognized his voice." Phil and Marcel were good friends. They visited each other's yards and sometimes went on walks together.

Norman scooped up the coffee grinds, orange peels, and crumpled paper. Suddenly he gasped. There, under a plastic bread wrapper, was a long, narrow bone. There were shreds of bloodied flesh clinging to it. There were deep marks on one end, where someone—or *something*—had sunk its teeth.

It was hideous.

Norman jumped away from it with a little shriek. Milo rolled over to see what had scared Norman.

"Look at that!" Norman said. "It's horrible!"

"It's a bone, Norman," Milo said.

Phil jumped straight into the air, trying to snatch the bone.

"But what kind of a bone?" Norman asked,

staring at it. "And where's the rest of the body it came from?"

"For Pete's sake, Norman, it's a steak bone," Milo said. "And the rest of the body it came from is probably still in the butcher shop."

"I don't think it's a steak bone," Norman whispered. He felt a tingle down his neck. "I think it's a human bone."

CHAPTER 3

"Hello, boys."

Norman and Milo looked up. Mrs. Lana Rosenbloom was standing in the doorway, leaning on her cane. "Oh, my, Marcel must have gotten out again last night."

"We'll take care of it, Mrs. Rosenbloom," said Milo. He scooped up some scattered coffee grounds with a plastic jar lid.

Phil leaped for the bone again.

"What's got Phil so excited?" asked Mrs. Rosenbloom.

"He wants this." Norman held up the bone. Mrs. Rosenbloom limped down the steps to the sidewalk.

"How odd," she said.

"It was in your garbage," Norman said. "Phil, sit!" he ordered as Phil shot into the air, snapping at the bone.

"From our garbage?" Mrs. Rosenbloom looked puzzled. "That's a meat bone. We had fish last night."

"You didn't throw this out?" Norman asked.

"No." Mrs. Rosenbloom shook her head. "I can't imagine how it got there."

But Norman could.

"Maybe Marcel went through someone else's garbage and brought it home with him," said Milo. He picked up the last bits of orange rind and placed the cover back on the can.

Mrs. Rosenbloom groaned. "Just what we need!" she said. "Someone else's garbage."

They're wrong, thought Norman. Marcel's poodle teeth could never have made those hideous, deep fang marks.

"Thank you for cleaning up," Mrs. Rosenbloom said. "Would you boys like some lemonade?"

"Sure," said Milo.

"Come around back. Norman, throw that bone away. Heaven knows where it came from."

Norman knew where it came from. It came from some poor, unfortunate person who had happened upon a savage wolf in the moonlight.

The boys and the two Mrs. Rosenblooms sipped lemonade and watched Marcel and Phil frisk around the yard.

Norman asked the sisters if they had heard the howling during the night.

"I didn't hear a thing," said Mrs. Lola.

"You don't hear very well anyway," said Mrs. Lana. "And you don't wear your hearing aid at night."

"Did you hear it?" her twin asked.

"No, but the air conditioner was on," Mrs. Lana said. "I can't hear anything outside when it's running."

"I suppose it could have been Marcel," said Mrs. Lola. "After all, he did get out. And he's been acting so strange lately."

"Strange?" Norman put his glass down. "What do you mean?"

"Sort of restless and irritable," said Mrs. Lana. "It's hard to explain. He's just not himself."

"He paces back and forth all the time," added Mrs. Lola. "He can't seem to sit still. And he keeps getting out at night. We don't know how he manages it."

"Do you lock your dog door?" Norman asked.

"Sometimes we forget to."

"We don't have a dog door," Mrs. Lola said.

Norman looked across the yard. Phil and Marcel had started a tug of war with something. Suddenly there was a low, threatening growl. Phil let go and squirmed backward on his belly till he was up against the fence.

"Marcel!" scolded Mrs. Lana. "That's no way to behave with your friend." Leaning on her cane, she moved as fast as she could toward the fence.

Mrs. Lana took Marcel's collar and pulled. Marcel's lip curled back, and his sharp white teeth glistened in the sunlight. Another rumbling growl came from his throat.

Norman shuddered at the sound, and at the sight of Marcel's fangs. Phil snatched the thing they'd been tugging at and raced across the yard. He leaped into Norman's arms.

"What is that?" Milo asked as Norman pulled the thing from Phil's mouth. "Yuck, it's a mess."

It was a small, plastic baby doll. One eye was missing. One arm had been ripped off. Its little white bonnet was in shreds. There was a jagged slash across its tummy.

Norman went cold with horror. "It's been

mangled, he said hoarsely. "Just like little Angel's Baby Bootsie doll."

"What are you talking about?" Milo demanded.

"In *Red Fang, Dog of Darkness,*" Norman said. "Don't you remember?"

Mrs. Lola took a look at the doll and shook her head. "Now where did that come from?" she wondered.

Mrs. Lana was leading Marcel into the house. "Probably the same place he found the bone. What is the matter with you, Marcel? You're so touchy these days."

Norman, trembling, held Phil against his chest. Phil's heart was beating even faster than his own.

"Well, I guess the wolf hunt is over," Milo said.

"I think," Norman whispered, "we might be hunting a different kind of wolf."

CHAPTER 4

"Norman," said his mother several days later, "why are you picking all the frankfurters out of the Frankfurters Florentine? You like frankfurters."

"I'm not picking out the frankfurters," Norman said. "I'm picking out the Florentine."

"Florentine," Norman had just discovered, meant spinach. Mrs. Newman had a catering business. Whenever she had food left over from a party, it usually showed up at the Newmans' dinner table.

She had catered a big Fourth of July barbecue a week ago. A soaking rain had cut the party short, and the Newmans had been eating Hot Dogs Oriental, Hot Dogs á la Grecque, and Sweet and Sour Hot Dogs for days.

Elaine, meanwhile, was eating the spinach, the rice, and the tomatoes, dropping the frankfurter slices onto her napkin.

Norman's mother looked at the little heap of meat. "I suppose you're a vegetarian again?" she said. Winona McCall was a vegetarian, and Elaine seemed to become a vegetarian every time there was something she didn't like for dinner.

"I don't see why that surprises you, Mother," she said. "If I don't believe in killing animals for their fur, I don't see why we should kill them for their flesh."

She lifted one of the four glasses of water in front of her. "Besides," she added, "all this water is very filling."

She looked up at the kitchen clock. "It's almost seven!" She pushed her chair back. "*The Werewolf of Wall Street* is on in two minutes!"

"*The Werewolf of Wall Street?*" Norman repeated. "You want to watch a werewolf movie?"

"It's one of Winona McCall's earliest films," Elaine explained. "She has a small but crucial role as a spunky secretary."

"If it's a really small part," Norman said, "I'll watch it with you."

"Oh, goody," Elaine said sourly.

"Clear the table first," their mother said. But Elaine and Norman were in the den before she could finish the sentence.

"It's funny that a werewolf movie should be on tonight," Norman said. "Because—"

"Shh! If you want to watch with me, you have to be absolutely quiet."

"This is TTN," said a deep-voiced announcer, "the Total Terror Network—all scary, all the time."

"I'm not cleaning this kitchen by myself!" their mother called.

"Then come watch the movie with us," Norman called back.

His mother walked into the den. "That's not exactly what I had in mind," she said.

The Total Terror Network was showing some clips from the upcoming movie. "This stockbroker really made a killing in the market!" the announcer exclaimed.

"Cute," said Mrs. Newman.

"Isn't he?" Elaine sighed. She was gazing at the star, Kirk Blackburn. "Jeff Donohue looks just like him."

"Who's Jeff Donohue?" her mother asked.

"Just some boy."

"You know," Norman tried again, "I've been

thinking about that wolf—"

"Shh!" Elaine said. "It's starting."

Norman had seen werewolf movies before, but *The Werewolf of Wall Street* was definitely the most gruesome. Kirk Blackburn played a rich stockbroker who turned into a wolf whenever the moon was full or he wanted to take over a new corporation.

Winona McCall played his secretary, who became suspicious when her boss's enemies started turning up dead on the floor of the stock exchange.

Kirk really loved Winona, but when she figured out his secret, he had to kill her. He bit her throat and threw her off the top of the World Trade Center. He didn't really want to do it. Just before she died, he told her sadly, "The werewolf always kills the thing he loves the most."

Elaine leaned forward to watch Winona McCall plunge to her death. As soon as she hit the sidewalk, Elaine stood up and headed for the door.

"Don't you want to see the rest of the movie?" Norman asked.

"What for? I just wanted to watch Winona McCall's part."

"Good," said her mother. "Then you can take care of the dishes. This movie is kind of fun."

"But it's not very realistic," Norman said.

"How could it be realistic?" Mrs. Newman laughed. "It's about werewolves."

After the movie, Norman went to his room to finish the last few pages of *Red Fang, Dog of Darkness*. But he found it hard to concentrate, even though Monroe Marlin was his favorite author and *Red Fang* was the best book he'd ever read.

For the past few days, all he could think about was Marcel: the way he'd growled at Phil and how Mrs. Rosenbloom and Mrs. Rosenbloom said he'd been acting so strangely.

And the mysterious bone with the hideous fang marks and the jagged bits of flesh still stuck to it— a bone that was in the Rosenblooms' garbage even though the Rosenblooms had never seen it before.

And the savagely mangled doll in the yard. Finding the dismembered Baby Bootsie doll had been Timmy's first clue that Red Fang was no ordinary Irish setter.

And the howling, and the shadowy animal Norman had seen slinking around the corner in the moonlight.

There hadn't been any howling since then. But two nights it had rained, and two nights were foggy, so the moon hadn't shone.

Maybe *The Werewolf of Wall Street* wasn't a very realistic movie. But they'd gotten one thing right. The one thing that everyone knows for sure about werewolves.

When the moon comes out . . . so do they.

false

I hate candy

I have cavaties

$4 \frac{1}{2} = 90$ ✓

$\frac{1}{2} = 10$ ✓

$2 = 40$ ✓

$1 \frac{1}{2} = 30$ ✓

CHAPTER 5

Norman couldn't sleep. He felt like he'd been lying in bed for hours.

He had it all figured out, and it was all horribly clear.

Marcel was a werewolf. Norman knew it was unusual for a dog to turn into a wolf. Except for Red Fang, all the werewolves Norman had ever heard about had started out as humans.

He turned on the bedside lamp and looked at his clock. Five minutes to midnight. Elaine and his mother had gone to bed a long time ago. They were probably sound asleep. They had no idea of the terrible danger that lurked across the street.

He got out of bed and went to his bookcase. He pulled out a book his Aunt Deborah had given him.

It was called *Everything You Always Wanted To Know About Werewolves*. *Red Fang, Dog of Darkness* was a story that Monroe Marlin had made up. But Aunt Deborah's book was nonfiction. It was a scientific study of werewolves and their habits.

If a dog could become a werewolf, this book should certainly mention it.

Norman turned to the index. He ran his finger down the column, looking for "Dogs as Werewolves." There was no listing for dogs. Maybe he should look under "Animals as Werewolves." He went back to the beginning of the index.

"OW-OOO!"

"Yipes!" Norman dropped the book. It landed on his bare toe.

"Ow!"

"OW-OOO!"

He hopped to the window. But with the light on he couldn't see anything. He hopped over to the night table and turned off the lamp. He heard a little whimper from the bed. In the moonlight, he could see Phil's stubby tail sticking out from under the pillow.

"You're not afraid, are you, Phil?" Norman asked. Phil's tail disappeared all the way under the pillow.

Norman went to the window and looked across the street. There were no garbage cans in front of the Rosenblooms' tonight, and no Marcel, either.

He looked up the street in the other direction. Nothing.

Maybe Marcel was howling from inside the house.

"OW-OOO-OOO!"

He can't be inside, Norman told himself. *That's too loud.*

He shoved his bare feet into his sneakers. "Come on Phil. We're going on a werewolf hunt."

The pillow moved, but Phil didn't come out from under it.

"I know it's scary." Norman reached under the pillow and scooped Phil up. "But we have to do it. People's lives are in danger."

"Woof!" Phil protested, trying to scramble out of Norman's grasp.

"Yeah, you're right," Norman said. "Dogs' lives, too."

Norman carried Phil into the kitchen and snapped his leash on.

I ought to have some kind of weapon, Norman thought. *This could be dangerous. If Marcel realizes I'm onto him, he might try to get rid of me, just like the Werewolf of Wall Street got rid of Winona McCall.*

Norman looked around the kitchen. He needed something that would work from a distance, something that would give him time to run for safety if Marcel spotted him.

On the counter next to the stove there was a can of Sprat. It was a cooking spray that his mother used to grease frying pans and cake tins.

Perfect, thought Norman. It would work just like a flame thrower, except it would throw oil instead of flame. And it wouldn't hurt Marcel—just startle him and make him greasy.

He grabbed the can and tugged a very unwilling Phil out the back door.

Norman ran around to the front of the house. He looked up and down the street. It was silent and eerie in the moonlight.

He heard the howl again. Phil yipped and made a dash back toward the house, but Norman held onto the leash.

"Come on, Phil," he said. "You've got to come with me. I'm not allowed out this late by myself."

He picked up the dog and started walking toward the direction of the howling. "Maybe

Marcel's in his yard," he said. "If he can't get out, we won't have to worry."

Carrying Phil in one arm and holding the Sprat in his other hand, Norman jogged down the street to the Rosenblooms' house. He tiptoed around the side of the garage and peered into the yard.

There was no sign of Marcel. "Maybe he's in his doghouse," Norman whispered. Marcel's doghouse was in the far corner of the yard under a large tree.

Norman knew he should look inside the doghouse. But it was so *dark* in that corner of the yard.

A cloud passed over the moon. Suddenly it looked like the tree was moving, its leaves twisting slowly, though the air was absolutely still.

Norman shivered. Then the cloud moved away from the moon, and he saw something hanging from the tree. He squinted, trying to make out what it was.

It looked black, and limp, and about the same size as Marcel.

"Oh, no," breathed Norman. "It can't be."

Was there another werewolf hunter in the neighborhood? One who knew how dogs could turn into werewolves? Had he gotten to Marcel before Norman had?

"I can't look," he whispered to Phil. "It's too horrible."

But if it was too horrible for Norman, what about Mrs. Rosenbloom and Mrs. Rosenbloom? How would they feel when they woke up in the morning and found their beloved Marcel's lifeless body hanging right next to his own doghouse?

Norman moaned softly. *They might faint,* he thought. *They might have heart attacks. They might never get over the shock.*

"We *have* to look," he told Phil. "We can't leave the body there for them to find."

Norman took a deep breath and tried to stop trembling. He put Phil down to undo the latch on the gate. Slowly he eased it open and moved into the yard. He held the Sprat can out in front of him, finger on the push button. Phil followed him, sniffing the ground.

Terrified of what he would see, Norman forced himself across the yard toward Marcel's doghouse. The closer he got to the tree, the slower he moved. He took the last few steps feeling as if his sneakers were made of lead.

Finally, standing right under the lowest branch of the tree, he reached up and tugged at the Thing.

It slid off the branch and fell over Norman's head. He gasped and struggled to pull it away from his face. It felt like curly fur. It smelled strange, like leather and musty basement.

"Yecchh!" Norman didn't know what the thing was, but it definitely wasn't a dead French poodle.

"AW-OOO!"

"Yipes!" The sound was so close, and so loud, that the creature had to be practically on top of him.

Suddenly, from out of the shadows behind the doghouse, *something* came streaking toward Norman. Phil the Wonder Dog barked once. Then he whirled around, raced across the yard, and out the gate.

"Phil!" Norman cried. The creature sprang toward him. It was lean and hairy and its eyes gleamed green-gold in the moonlight.

The werewolf! Norman was frozen with fear. He tried to scream and couldn't. He tried to turn and run, but couldn't.

It was almost on him now, just about to spring for his throat. Norman held up the Sprat and pushed the button.

"ACK!" A blast of oil hit him in the face. He staggered backward and dropped the can. The

werewolf veered around him and raced for the fence.

Frantically, Norman wiped at his eyes, not realizing he was using the furry thing as a handkerchief.

He cleared the spray out of his eyes just in time to see the werewolf leap over the fence and disappear into the night.

CHAPTER

6

By the time Norman and Phil got back to sleep, it was four in the morning. By the time Norman woke up, it was ten o'clock. He heard shouts and thumping noises coming from the living room.

He pulled on his clothes and stumbled sleepily out of his room. Elaine and her friend Deirdre were in the living room. They were jumping up and down, waving their arms and yelling.

"Don't kill foxes, don't kill minks!"

"Anyone who wears fur stinks!"

"What are you doing?" Norman asked.

"Practicing our anti-fur cheers," Elaine said. "What does it look like we're doing?"

"It looks like you're trying to stamp out a brush fire," Norman answered.

Elaine lunged for him, but Norman darted around a chair and escaped into the kitchen.

"Well, good morning," his mother said, looking up from her computer. "Aren't we the sleepyhead today?"

"I didn't get to sleep till four," Norman told her.

"For heaven's sake, why not?"

"Because of the werewolf."

She stared at him. "The were—you mean that silly movie scared you so badly?"

"Not the movie," he said. "The *real* werewolf."

His mother rolled her eyes. "Norman, I really don't have time for this. I promised the Fat Fighters of America I could cater their whole dinner using only seven grams of fat, and I can't find—"

"Mom, this could be very dangerous!" Norman cried.

"So can fat grams!"

"But Mom, I *saw*—"

"Norman, if you keep scaring yourself like this, I'm going to call the cable company and cancel TTN. And then I'm going to take every one of your horror books and lock them up until you're twenty-one." She turned back to her computer. "Now eat some breakfast before it's time for lunch."

Norman sighed. He took a bowl of cereal and headed back to his room. Elaine and Deirdre were still practicing cheers.

"Maybe we could do a human pyramid," Elaine said. "Jeff could hold us up on his shoulders."

"Both of us?" Deirdre said doubtfully.

"Well, just me, then." Elaine giggled.

Norman shut his door and put the cereal bowl down on the desk. He'd been so terrified after the werewolf attack that he'd almost forgotten he still had the weird thing he'd found in the tree.

Now, in the daytime, with Phil curled up asleep on it, the thing didn't look so weird. Norman bent down to examine it.

It looked like some kind of fur, but not like any Norman had ever seen.

Aunt Deborah had a fox coat with long, sleek fur and shiny silk lining on the inside. This fur was short and flat and knobby. It felt smooth, but looked bumpy. It was too small to be a coat, and there were no sleeves, so it couldn't be a jacket. Besides, it had no lining. It just had a soft, leathery feel, like . . . like . . . Norman tried to think of what it reminded him of.

"Oh!" he gasped. He jumped up, hitting his

head on the underside of his desk. "Ow!" Phil opened his eyes and yawned.

"Phil, get off that!" Norman cried.

Phil sniffed the black curly fur and began to nibble on a corner of it.

Norman backed away in horror. "Phil, no!" he wailed. "Don't you know what that is?"

> *In some countries, it is believed that werewolves shed their wolf skins and hang them on trees when they return to human form. Therefore, if you can find the skin of the werewolf and destroy it, he will never be able to change back into a werewolf again.*

There it was, in black and white, right on page eighteen of *Everything You Always Wanted To Know About Werewolves*. Werewolves could take off their fur coats to turn back into humans. So they must be able to take off their *human* coats when they turned into werewolves.

How could they get out of their human skin? Wouldn't it be messy? Wouldn't it be *disgusting*?

Maybe, Norman thought, *there's a zipper.*

But how they managed it wasn't important. The important thing was, if human werewolves

could change their skins, dog werewolves probably could, too. Which meant that the black, curly fur thing in Phil's mouth was Marcel's *dog skin!*

Norman could hardly keep from screaming as he ran down the hall and out the front door.

CHAPTER 7

Milo was shooting baskets in his driveway when Norman came barreling across the lawn.

Milo belonged to a wheelchair basketball team. They didn't have any league games in the summer, but Milo liked to stay in practice.

"Hey, Norman! Want to shoot some hoops?"

"There's no time for that," Norman said breathlessly. "Remember how I thought that howling we heard was a wolf?"

Milo nodded.

"Well, I was wrong," Norman said. "It's not a wolf."

"This doesn't come as a big shock to me, Norman."

"It's a *werewolf*."

"A werewolf!" Milo exclaimed.

"Shh!" Norman warned. "Keep your voice down. We don't want to start a panic."

"You're the only one panicking," Milo pointed out.

"That's because I'm the only one who knows," Norman said. "But if word gets out that Marcel is a werewolf—"

"Marcel, the French poodle?" Milo hugged the basketball to his chest, shaking with laughter.

"This is no laughing matter!"

"A poodle werewolf?" Milo gasped. "Wouldn't that be a weredog?"

"Milo, be serious! Mrs. Rosenbloom and Mrs. Rosenbloom are in terrible danger! The werewolf always kills the thing he loves the most!"

"You watched that movie, too?" Milo tossed the basketball toward the hoop. It bounced off the garage door. Norman caught it on the rebound and tucked it firmly under one arm.

"This has nothing to do with a movie!" Norman said. "This is real life I'm talking about."

"Give me the ball, Norman."

"Not until you listen to me."

Milo wheeled toward him. "First of all," he said, "if there is such a thing as werewolves, they're humans that turn into wolves. Not dogs."

"Not always," said Norman. "What about Red Fang, Dog of Darkness?"

"Norman, *Red Fang* is a *story*. Monroe Marlin made it up. Give me the ball."

"Monroe Marlin didn't make up what happened to me last night," Norman said dramatically. "What I saw was no story."

Norman kept moving as Milo rolled toward him. The words tumbled out of him in a rush as he described how the howling had woken him up, how he'd followed the sound to the Rosenblooms' yard, and how the werewolf had charged him, with glittering eyes and bared fangs, thirsty for his blood.

"Are you sure it wasn't Marcel? Maybe you were so scared you just thought you saw a wolf."

"A werewolf," Norman corrected him. "And it *was* Marcel. That's what I'm trying to tell you. It was Marcel in his werewolf skin. He had long, hairy fur like a wolf."

"Hmm." Milo thought about it for a minute. "Maybe it was some other dog."

"How could another dog have gotten in Marcel's yard?" Norman asked. "The gate was closed."

"Well, you saw it jump over the fence," Milo said.

"But wouldn't Marcel have barked or run after him?"

Milo frowned. "Probably. Dogs are very protective about their territory."

He thought for a moment.

"Maybe Marcel was inside the house," Milo said, "so he couldn't get out to chase the other dog away."

"But he would have heard the other dog—I mean, the werewolf," Norman said. "He would have barked like crazy."

"Yeah, I guess he would have." Milo frowned again. "All right, Norman. Something's weird. But whatever it is, it has nothing to do with werewolves."

"I have proof," Norman said.

"Proof that Marcel is a werewolf?"

Norman nodded.

"What kind of proof?" Milo demanded.

"I have his skin."

"*Whose* skin?" asked Milo.

"Marcel's. Marcel's dog skin."

Milo stared at him in disbelief. "You're telling me that Marcel is running around without his skin?"

"He's not running around without his skin," Norman interrupted. "He's running around in his werewolf outfit."

"Give me the basketball," Milo said.

"Not till you see my proof," Norman said.

"Norman, you had proof that our teacher was a space alien. You had proof that Elaine put a spell on you. I've seen your proof before. Now, give me the ball."

Norman turned and started to run toward his house. "Come and get it," he yelled. All he had to do was show his friend Marcel's dog skin. Once Milo saw it, he'd realize that Norman was right.

Milo chased after him, rolling his chair across the driveway and over the Newmans' lawn.

He got to the front steps and stopped. Norman darted into the house.

"No fair!" Milo yelled. "You know I can't get up the steps."

Norman was heading for his room to get Marcel's skin when he ran smack into Elaine. She and Deirdre were carrying a bunch of posters.

"Watch where you're going, fleabrain," Elaine snarled.

"I need help getting Milo's wheelchair in," he said breathlessly.

"Okay, okay," Elaine grumbled. Norman knew she wouldn't refuse. She liked Milo. "But it better not take too long. We're busy."

"It's two steps," said Norman. "How long can it take?"

Norman tossed the basketball into his room and went back outside. Elaine and Deirdre were already hoisting Milo's chair up the entry steps. Milo wheeled himself into the house.

"Thanks," he said.

"No problem," Elaine said, much more nicely than she ever spoke to Norman. The girls went into Elaine's room with their posters.

Milo glared at Norman. "Now *give me that basketball*."

"It's in my room," Norman said. He lowered his voice. "So is Marcel's skin. Come on."

"Oh, all right." Milo followed him down the hall.

Norman stood at the doorway of his room. "It's right there." He pointed. "Under the desk."

Milo wheeled himself over to the desk. He bent down and picked up the black, curly skin.

"This is weird," he muttered. "You know something, Norman? This really does feel sort of like Marcel's coat. Except it's pretty greasy."

"That's because it *is* Marcel's coat," Norman said. "With some Sprat on it."

"It can't be," he said.

"Then what is it?" Norman challenged him.

"I don't know what it is," Milo said slowly. "But we'd better find out what it isn't."

CHAPTER

8

"We'll just ring the bell and ask one of the Mrs. Rosenblooms if they need anything," Milo said as they headed down the street. "Marcel will come to the door, and we'll see he's fine, and then we'll know that can't be his skin."

"Their garbage cans aren't out," Norman said as they crossed the street. "And it's pickup day."

"Maybe they forgot," Milo said.

"Or maybe they couldn't put the cans out," Norman said darkly. "Because the werewolf killed the ones he loved the most."

"Well, we'll find out in a minute."

Norman and Milo went up the front walk. Norman rang the doorbell. They waited.

No one answered. Norman leaned his ear

against the door. He couldn't hear a sound.

"Ring it again," Milo said. "Mrs. Rosenbloom is pretty hard of hearing."

"But the other Mrs. Rosenbloom isn't," said Norman. He pressed the bell hard three times. He knocked on the door loudly.

No one came.

"I knew it!" he said. "Marcel killed them!"

"They could be out shopping," Milo said.

Norman ran to the garage and looked through the window. He saw the Rosenblooms' big green Cadillac.

"Without their car?"

"Mmm," said Milo. "Maybe they went on a trip. It's summertime. People go away in the summer."

"And maybe they're dead or injured from a werewolf attack!" Norman said. "And nobody knows but us. We have to *do* something."

"I guess we could call the police and ask them to check the house," Milo said.

"Yes!" said Norman. "That's what we should—"

They heard a horn behind them. Norman turned. His mother's car pulled up next to the curb. She leaned out the window.

"Come on, Norman. It's time to pick up your father at the airport."

"I can't go," Norman said. "I have to—"

"Elaine's at the mall," she said, "and I don't want to leave you alone."

"But—"

"Go ahead," Milo said. "I'll call the police."

"You will?" Norman said. "You believe me this time?"

"I don't exactly believe you," Milo said. "But something's not right."

"Norman, let's go!" his mother said sharply.

"Okay, okay," he said, and jumped into the car.

Norman was always glad when his father came home from his trips. Sometimes he brought Norman and Elaine little gifts, but it wasn't the gifts that Norman looked forward to. And it wasn't just that Mrs. Newman made special dinners, sometimes without even using party leftovers.

Though Norman was really eager for a meal without frankfurters.

But his father wasn't as impatient as his mother about Norman's love for Monroe Marlin stories. He listened when Norman described the weird things that he'd seen. Mr. Newman didn't usually agree that the mysterious events were terribly mysterious. But he'd never threatened to take away Norman's books or cancel the cable.

Today though, Norman could hardly concentrate on his father's homecoming. He was too worried about Mrs. Rosenbloom and Mrs. Rosenbloom.

His father's plane had landed twenty minutes early. He was already waiting for them when they got to the terminal.

He hugged Norman and Mrs. Newman. He picked up his carry-on bag and held out something that looked like a six-pack of soda.

"See what I brought Elaine from Cincinnati." He grinned.

Norman took the carton from him and read the label. "Cincinnati Seltzer—the Water That Made Ohio Famous."

"Of course," his father added, "at the rate she drinks water, this ought to last about eight hours."

Mr. Newman reached into his pocket. "I brought you a souvenir, too, Norman." He pulled out something small and shiny on a long chain.

"What is it?" Norman turned it over in his hands.

"The company I visited is called Bullitt-Silverman. They have a softball team named the Silver Bullets. This is their team emblem."

"Wow." Norman put the chain around his neck. "Is it a real bullet?"

"I don't know," said Mr. Newman. "Why? Do you want to kill a werewolf?"

"Lenny!" Mrs. Newman looked furious.

Norman's father spread his arms out. "What? I was just joking."

Norman looked at him, his eyes wide. "How did you know about the werewolf?"

CHAPTER 9

When they got home, the light on the phone answering machine was flashing.

"Three messages," Mrs. Newman said. "We haven't been out that long."

"I'm going to Milo's," Norman said. "I have to find out—"

"Just a minute, Norman," his mother said. "I'm not finished talking to you."

"You talked to me all the way home!"

He had told his parents about all the suspicious things he'd found tracking the werewolf. He told them how he'd seen the werewolf with his own eyes.

He didn't tell them that he'd seen the werewolf at midnight. He didn't think it was important to mention the time he'd seen it, just that he *did* see it.

They were not convinced. But they agreed it would be a good idea to make sure that the Mrs. Rosenblooms were all right.

Norman's father thought a French poodle werewolf sounded pretty funny.

Norman's mother was not amused.

"One of these days," she warned him, "something really will happen, and no one will believe you. Just like the boy who cried wolf."

"You mean the boy who cried werewolf." Mr. Newman chuckled.

"Lenny! Don't encourage him." She pressed the button on the phone machine. The Evil Elaine's voice shrieked from the speaker.

"Mom! Come to the mall as soon as you get home. They won't let me go!"

"Wow!" Norman said. "She's finally gotten arrested!"

"Oh, no!" his mother cried. There was a little beep, and the second message began to play.

"Mom! Where *are* you?" Elaine's voice was even shriller. "You've got to get me out of here." Then, much softer, like she was whispering into the phone: "They won't even let me use the *bathroom*."

"Let's go," Mr. Newman said.

"We don't even know where in the mall she is," Norman's mother said.

"They've probably got her in the security office. We can find out—"

Another beep. "Mrs. Lincoln, this is Officer Beamish, chief of Sunset Mall Security. If you're not down here by one, we're going to have to call the police and the juvenile authorities to pick up Mary Todd."

"Who's Mrs. Lincoln?" Norman asked. "Who's Mary Todd?"

"Good grief," his father said. "She gave them a phony name."

The message was still running: ". . . very serious arson charges."

"Arson!" wailed Norman's mother.

"Come *on*!" Mr. Newman grabbed her arm. "It's almost one now."

Norman raced out to the car with them.

"Maybe you'd better stay at Milo's," his mother said frantically.

"No way!" Norman jumped into the backseat. "I want to see Elaine get arrested."

His father groaned and started the car.

"She was just going to demonstrate," Norman's mother said as they zoomed out of the driveway.

"They were practicing these silly cheerleading routines before they left. How did she get involved with arson?"

"Maybe she burned down Murray's Mansion of Mink," Norman suggested.

Mrs. Newman put her hand over her eyes. "When that girl gets out of jail," she vowed, "I will kill her."

The security office was on the lower level of the mall. Elaine was slumped in an orange plastic chair, looking sullen.

One of her posters was on the floor at her feet. It was half burned. All Norman could read was,

"FUR

"PET I

"DON'T WE

"Where have you been?" Elaine shrieked. "Deirdre's mother picked her up hours ago!"

A large man in a green jacket and checked pants was perched on the edge of a desk opposite Elaine. A plastic name plate on his jacket pocket read: "Fred Beamish, Chief of Security." There was a large bottle of aspirin next to him.

"Mrs. Lincoln?" He slid off the desk and came toward them. "Mr. Lincoln?"

"Uh, well, actually—" Norman's father cleared his throat.

"We're her parents," Norman's mother cut in quickly. "Why are you holding her here?"

"And how come you didn't handcuff her?" Norman asked.

"Shut up, you little troublemaker!" Elaine snarled.

"I'm not the one who's in trouble," Norman pointed out.

"You will be when I get you alone."

The officer put his arms behind his back and eyed Elaine. "Pretty violent, isn't she?"

"No, she's not!" Mrs. Newman said. "Now, what is it that she's accused of doing?"

"She set a fire in front of Murray's Mansion of Mink," the man said sternly. "She endangered the lives of every shopper in the mall."

"It was a tiny little fire!" Elaine said. "And we stamped it out before it spread."

"Elaine, why would you do such a thing?" her father asked.

"Elaine?" said the security chief. "She told me her name was Mary. Mary Todd."

"It was a protest," Elaine said. "But after Jeff left, there were only two of us."

"Who's Jeff?" her father asked.

"Just some boy," Mrs. Newman said sarcastically. "Go on."

"He said he had to go home and groom his dog." Elaine shook her head in disgust. "Do you believe it? Grooming his stupid dog was more important than—"

"Elaine!" her father interrupted. "What about the fire?"

"Well, nobody was paying any attention to us. And hardly anybody was going into Murray's anyway."

"But didn't you want people not to buy fur?" her father asked.

"Of course," said Elaine. "But we wanted them not to buy it because of our demonstration. Not just because they weren't going to buy it in the first place."

Mr. Beamish reached for the aspirin bottle.

"The fire, Elaine," her father reminded her. "Get to the part about the fire."

"We had to get people to notice us," she said. "We had to do something *dramatic*. So we set fire to the fur. Then they noticed us, all right."

"What fur?" her mother asked. "Where did you get a fur?"

Mr. Beamish pulled out something from behind the desk. It was black and charred and smelly. "This is what she set fire to."

Norman needed only a glance to see what the black, burned thing was.

"Oh, no!" He smacked his forehead. "*Ow*. Do you know what you've done?" he yelled at Elaine.

"Norman, what's gotten into you?" his mother asked.

"That's Marcel's skin!" he wailed. "Now he'll have to be a werewolf *forever*!"

CHAPTER 10

"It's not Marcel's skin," Norman's mother insisted later that afternoon after they returned home. "It's a cape. And I still don't understand what you were doing with it."

"I found it in the Rosenblooms' yard," Norman said. "That's how I knew it was Marcel's dog skin. Elaine stole it from my room."

"I did not," she said. "I found it in *our* yard. Your stupid dog was chewing on it."

Phil wagged his tail. He recognized the word "dog." He probably didn't know what "stupid" meant.

"He must have pulled it out through the dog door," Mr. Newman said. He turned to Norman. "But why did you take it from the Rosenblooms?"

"I saw it hanging from a tree," Norman explained. "And then I was scared by the werewolf. I didn't know what it was till I got home. I was going to put it back tonight."

He glowered at the Evil Elaine. "But now that she's burned it, Marcel can never turn back into a dog again."

Norman's mother put her hand over her eyes. "I am very angry with both of you," she began. Her voice was dangerously soft.

"You," she told Elaine, "were very lucky to get off with just a warning. What you did was foolish and dangerous."

"And illegal," Norman added.

His mother glared at him. "*You* took something that didn't belong to you, which is now ruined. We'll have to pay for it."

"I didn't destroy it," Norman said. "*She* did. And don't you think there are more important things than money? Without that coat, Marcel will spend the rest of his life as a—"

"It's *not* Marcel's coat!" Mrs. Newman said furiously. "It's Persian lamb. My mother had a jacket just like it. Now stop this werewolf business!"

Norman touched the edge of the ruined cape. "You're sure?" he asked. "I never heard of a

Persian lamb. And it feels like a poodle."

"I'm sure," Mrs. Newman said. "It isn't very popular anymore, but it used to be back in the forties."

"You're going to have to go to the Rosenblooms and tell them what you did," Norman's father said.

"Mrs. Rosenbloom," Norman remembered, "and Mrs. Rosenbloom! We don't even know if they're alive!"

He dashed for the front door.

"Norman, you get back—"

"I have to talk to Milo!" He ran outside. He saw Milo wheeling full speed down the street, just as two police cars pulled up in front of the Rosenblooms' house.

"Milo!" he shouted.

Milo turned around. "I called them hours ago," he said. "I don't know what took them so long. Come *on*."

They raced to the Rosenblooms' house. Norman's parents and Elaine followed.

Four policemen were stepping out of the two cars as Norman and Milo got to the Rosenblooms'.

"I thought you'd never get here!" Milo said.

"Are you the boy who called?" one of the officers asked.

Milo nodded. "We haven't seen them for days, and they're old, and—"

Norman's parents and sister reached the group just in time to hear one of the two policemen explain.

"We would have been here sooner, but there was a disturbance at the mall."

Elaine took a few careful steps back from the group and turned her head away. Mrs. Newman, still carrying the Persian lamb cape, glared at her.

"Are you going to break the door down?" Norman asked.

"That's a little drastic," said the first policeman. "We'll ring the bell first."

Other neighbors were beginning to gather to see what the excitement was about. Milo's father and mother arrived.

"I've been here three times since I called you," Milo said. "They're not answering."

Just then a white taxi rounded the corner, honked its horn, and pulled into the Rosenblooms' driveway. MERCURY CAB: AIRPORT SERVICE was lettered on the back.

The back doors opened. A Mrs. Rosenbloom came out of each door. Marcel jumped out after them.

"Marcel!" cried Norman. The dog looked perfectly normal. His black poodle coat was in fine condition.

Phil woofed joyfully at the sight of his friend. The dogs ran toward each other, barking their hellos.

"What in the world is going on?" Mrs. Lana looked dazed.

"Are you all right?" Milo asked. "We were worried about you. You just disappeared."

"This boy called us," the first policeman said, "to report you missing."

"Oh, Milo," said Mrs. Lola. "I'm sorry you were worried. We're fine. A little sore from the donkey ride, that's all."

Norman stared at her. "*Donkey* ride?"

"Down the Grand Canyon," said Mrs. Lana.

Suddenly Mrs. Lola saw what Norman's mother was holding.

"My Persian lamb!" she said. "How did you get it?"

"Persian lamb?" Norman repeated. "Not poodle?"

Norman's mother, looking very embarrassed, held the cape out toward her.

"Oh, my goodness!" Mrs. Rosenbloom gasped.

"What happened to it?"

"It's a long story," Norman's mother began. "But we'll pay—"

At that moment, a large, hairy animal bounded around the corner and came racing up the street. It was long, and lean, and ran like the wind, its great jaws open.

"That's him!" Norman screamed. "That's the werewolf! Run for your lives!"

CHAPTER 11

The crowd scattered as the beast raced toward them.

"Quick!" Norman yanked the silver bullet from around his neck. He pressed it into the policeman's hand, then jumped up onto the hood of the taxi.

"Put it in your gun and shoot him!" he yelled. "A silver bullet is the only thing that can stop a werewolf!"

Marcel darted through the crowd and ran toward the animal.

"Marcel!" cried Mrs. Rosenbloom. "Marcel, come!"

"Phil!" Norman shouted as Phil trotted after Marcel.

The Evil Elaine started to laugh. She laughed so hard that she doubled over and clutched her stomach. "Werewolf!" she gasped. "That's no werewolf, you idiot! That's Tova."

Marcel and the hairy creature touched noses. Phil approached them and watched them nuzzle each other.

"Tova?" Norman stared at the three animals. "Who's Tova?"

Elaine struggled to catch her breath. "Jeff Donohue's dog. She's an Afghan hound."

"*The* Jeff Donohue?" her father asked.

"They just moved in around the corner," Elaine said. "He's the boy who demonstrated with us. Until he had to groom his dog."

"Well, he did a nice job on her," said Mr. Newman. "She's a fine-looking dog."

"It must have been Tova howling," Norman's mother said.

"Or Marcel," said Milo, "looking for Tova."

"No wonder Marcel has been acting so strangely," said Mrs. Rosenbloom, "and going out at night."

"And Tova must have been looking for Marcel the night Norman saw her," Milo said.

The second policeman took off his cap and

scratched his head. "I don't understand *any* of this."

"Hey, kid," the cab driver suddenly piped up. "Get down off my cab."

Norman scrambled down and went over to Milo. His head was swimming. Marcel wasn't a werewolf. Marcel's dog skin was only a fur cape.

But what about the mangled doll, and the bloody bone, and Tova's gleaming eyes as she streaked across the yard in the moonlight?

"That's it!" He leaned over to Milo. "*Tova's* the werewolf!" he whispered. "But if she bites Marcel, then he'll turn into a werewolf! And if Marcel bites Phil, *he'll* turn into a werewolf, too! And all the dogs in the neighborhood will—"

Milo sighed. "Give it up, Norman. There's no werewolf. But you sure had me going for awhile."

The neighbors were beginning to return home. Two of the policemen got into a car and drove off. The cab driver took the last pieces of luggage out of the trunk and set them down in the driveway.

Mrs. Rosenbloom and Mrs. Rosenbloom were talking to the two remaining policemen.

"So when our nieces couldn't go, they called us at the last minute and asked if we wanted to go instead. The tour was nonrefundable."

"And it gets pretty cold there at night," Mrs. Lola went on. "So I dug up my old Persian lamb cape and put it outside to air. It smelled just terrible."

"It was a real spur of the moment trip," said Mrs. Lana. "The next morning, we were in such a rush, Lola forgot all about the cape."

"I didn't remember it until we'd taken Marcel to the boarding kennel," said Mrs. Lola. "It was too late to come back and get it."

"That's why we didn't see Marcel around, either," Milo told Norman. "See? There's a reasonable explanation for everything."

"I still don't trust Tova," Norman muttered.

Milo's father and the cab driver carried the Rosenblooms' suitcases into the house. The policeman handed Norman back his silver bullet.

"I don't think we'll be needing this," he said.

"I'm not so sure—" Norman began.

"*Norman!*" His mother put her hand on his shoulder. Hard.

CHAPTER 12

"I don't understand it," Mrs. Newman said the next afternoon. "It's always right here, next to the stove."

"What's always right there?" Norman asked, peering into the refrigerator.

"The Sprat. I'm making crepes for the Fat Fighters of America dinner. The batter's ready, but I can't find the Sprat."

Norman shut the refrigerator door and quietly left the kitchen.

He passed Elaine on the way to his room. She was carrying a bottle of Cincinnati Seltzer. She looked even paler than usual.

"I think Mom's going to need you to go to the store," Norman said.

"Why can't you go?" Elaine scowled.

"I'm busy."

"Hunting werewolves?" she sneered.

"I'll catch one before you catch Jeff Donohue," he taunted.

"Little slug!" she hissed.

"Big slugess." He darted into his room and slammed the door.

He *was* busy. Just that morning he had gotten the new Monroe Marlin book. It was called *Mall of the Living Dead*. On the cover was a picture of three teenagers in a video arcade. They were dressed in tattered black clothes. They had ghastly white faces and long, thin fingers.

Under the title it said: "*Attention shoppers! You may get more than you bargained for when ZOMBIES invade the mall!*"

Norman had checked a bunch of other books out of the library, too: *Your Friend, the Ozone Layer; Sparky, the Chipmunk Who Thought He Was a Dog;* and *How to Make Big Money With Your Home Video Camera*.

He didn't plan to read any of them. He didn't even own a video camera. But he thought it was a good idea to sandwich *Mall of the Living Dead* in between some others in case his mother asked what he was reading.

He was already on page thirty. The book was really scary. It was about a group of teenagers who liked to hang out at the mall.

One spring day they went on a picnic near a cemetery. When they returned home that night, they were different.

Terribly different. . . .

Norman shivered as he picked up the book again. Those faces were so gruesome. And the clawlike hands seemed to be reaching right out of the cover at him.

"Hey." One of the girl zombies caught his eye. She had long, dark hair. Her eyes were like black coals. She was as thin and pale as Elaine.

"Hey." The closer he looked, the more he could see the resemblance.

"Holy cow," he whispered to Phil. "This zombie looks just like the Evil Elaine."

Elaine was extremely pale. Elaine always wore black. Elaine had long, thin fingers.

And Elaine had been spending almost every day at the mall.

"Yipes!"

Norman felt for the silver bullet on the chain

around his neck. He turned it over and over in his fingers, watching the way it glinted in the sunlight.

"Do you think," he asked Phil in a shaky voice, "this works for zombies, too?"